No giant or dragon

is bigger or stronger

than the human imagination.

—M. E.

For my parents, who took me to see Don Quixote's windmills

in La Mancha, Spain, when I was young

—M. E.

In memory of Uncle Frank, who dreamed my dream before I did

—R. C.

Author Acknowledgments
I thank God for stories, especially the quixotic ones. I am profoundly grateful
to my family and to Teresa Mlawer, Michelle Humphrey, Margaret Quinlin,
and the entire Peachtree publishing team.

Published by
PEACHTREE PUBLISHERS
1700 Chattahoochee Avenue
Atlanta, Georgia 30318-2112
www.peachtree-online.com

Text © 2017 by Margarita Engle
Illustrations © 2017 by Raúl Colón

Edited by Margaret Quinlin and Vicky Holifield
Design and composition by Nicola Simmonds Carmack

The illustrations were rendered in pen and ink and watercolor.

Printed in February 2017 by Tien Wah Press in Malaysia
10 9 8 7 6 5 4 3 2 1
First Edition
ISBN 978-1-56145-856-1

PHOTO CREDITS
Shutterstock
Illustration by Gustave Doré (Nicku), *Bronze sculpture by Lorenzo Coullault Valera in Madrid* (JPF),
Painting by Pablo Picasso (imageZebra)

Cataloging-in-Publication Data is available from the Library of Congress.

Miguel's Brave Knight

Young Cervantes and His Dream of Don Quixote

Poems by
Margarita Engle

Illustrated by
Raúl Colón

Ω
PEACHTREE
ATLANTA

Happiness

When I close my eyes,

I ride up high

on a horse the color

of moonrise!

But then I open my eyes,

and all I see is Papá, selling

the last of the horses from his stable—

his sweet old swaybacked nag,

a tired animal that would be happy

to sleep

all day.

With eyes shut tight again, I picture

a galloping steed

that will carry

Papá's sadness

away...

Stories

With my sisters

it's easy to pretend

that the tales Mamá tells

are real.

We act out each scene,

creating little plays filled with dragons

and heroes.

I wear Papá's barber bowl on my head

and hold Mamá's broom high.

I am a knight on a steed,

armed with a golden helmet

and glowing lance.

Happiness surrounds me as I prance

and gallop into my fanciful world

of brave deeds.

Hunger

To forget his troubles,

Papá often gambles away

his meager earnings.

And now he has been arrested!

Soldiers whisk him away

to be punished in debtors' prison

for borrowing money

that he cannot repay.

Without him, Mamá loses

furniture

silverware

hope.

They even took our beds and plates.

Where will we sleep?

How will we eat?

Comfort

Bare rooms.

Blank walls.

Our empty house looks

so spooky

and stark…

But when I close my eyes,

the spark of a story flares up.

A tale about a brave knight

who will ride out on

a strong horse

and right

all the wrongs

of this confusing

world.

Waiting

Papá is still in prison.

Mamá learns to survive.

To earn enough to feed us,

she buys and sells blankets

and trinkets, reads contracts,

signs papers,

works hard…

Meanwhile, at school, I daydream

as the teacher reads solemn tales

of ancient sorrows.

In my mind, the stories of wars

and more wars

swirl and twist away, to make room

for a brave man

who rides his horse

into a world

of exciting adventures!

Starting Over

Papá is finally free, so our family moves on.

We see new places,

new faces, new hopes!

At festivals, costumed actors

perform dazzling plays,

while magicians and musicians

astonish crowds

of strangers.

When storytellers on street corners

offer tales of giants and dragons, I imagine

telling my own stories someday, adventures

of a knight who roams toward a deep

blue lake…

a towering mountain…

a glittering

cave…

School

Sometimes I can go to school.

Our teacher reads us wondrous words from long ago.

If only there were enough books

for every student to open

those door-shaped

pages.

But only the teachers

are allowed to hold the books.

So I sit still and listen

with empty hands

and a head

full of wishes.

Smoke

Out in the plaza, I sniff

dark air.

A huge pile of books…
the sad scent
of each fiery
flare!

When I ask Mamá
why they are burning these books,
she says it is against the law to write
stories from one's imagination.
But how can anyone burn precious books
when our school has so few, and my mind
craves so many?

My brave knight

would rescue the flaming pages.

If Only

Papá works, cuts hair, trims beards,

pulls teeth, and treats injuries.

If only he did not gamble so much,

losing our money again and again

on card games, jousting,

and horse races.

If only we did not have to move so often.

If only we could live in my world

of brave

daydreams.

Daydreams

My daydreamed knight

protects farmers and maidens

from ogres, goblins, and trolls.

He sees windmills as giants

with enormous, spinning arms.

In his eyes, a frumpy milkmaid is

a beautiful princess. When he comes upon

a flock of sheep with long, curly wool,

he cries out, "Look! Look! Beware those

warriors wearing armor

made of snakes!"

With his chubby friend riding beside him

on a clumsy donkey,

my daydreamed knight

makes me

smile.

Disaster

No more smiles.

This is a plague year.

Disease.

Famine.

Terror.

No school.

No teacher.

No books.

Just sorrowful

prayers.

But I still carry invisible stories

in my head, my daydreamed tales

help calm

my worries.

Learning to Write

We move yet again.

This time, we reach Sevilla,

a great city of huge cathedrals,

wealthy cousins,

and a school for me.

My new teacher shows me

how to write

my own plays,

my own poems!

Now, each time I daydream, I imagine

an audience out in the plaza—farmers,

weavers, bakers, children—all watching,

listening, and smiling,

as I tell them tales

of my brave,

hopeful knight.

Hoping

Unpaid debts destroy our family's peace again.

Angry collectors threaten to send Papá

back to prison

in chains.

We sneak away at night,

running toward Madrid,

hoping for a future

free

of fear.

Where can we find such an impossible future?

Only inside the pages of my

imagination?

A New Life

I am older now.

In Madrid, I study with a teacher

who chooses four of my poems,

to be published in a book.

A real book, solid and heavy in my hands,

powerful and permanent, with pages

shaped

like open

doorways.

Some daydreams really do

come true.

Imagination

At last I feel confident enough

to dream of someday writing

the dazzling, adventurous story

of my own brave knight, who I will call

Don Quixote.

I will send him forth boldly

from my imagination

to right

all the wrongs

of this wonderful

but terribly

mixed-up

world.

Author's Note

Like many Latino children, I grew up surrounded by images of Don Quixote. My Cuban mother told me stories about his adventures, and my American father painted many pictures of the knight in various moods.

I grew up in the sixties, a time of great political and social turmoil. We heard daily news reports about the Cold War, the quest for free speech, the feminist movement, and the civil rights struggle. At home in Los Angeles, my family often participated in peace demonstrations and protests.

In 1965, when I was thirteen, we traveled to Spain to see the windmills that inspired Cervantes. In the remote hills of La Mancha, my father placed a bowl on his head, picked up a stick, and acted out the most famous scene from the book, in which Don Quixote attacks the windmills, foolishly thinking they are giants.

But there was so much more to the brave knight. There was also determination, perseverance, and above all, limitless hope, even in the face of ridicule. Don Quixote never gave up, even when discouraged. His idealism seemed relevant then, just as it does today.

Instead of retelling the stories of this brave knight, though, I chose to introduce you to the story of Miguel de Cervantes, the man who dreamed Don Quixote into existence.

Chief among my sources on the life of Cervantes was Donald McCrory's *No Ordinary Man: The Life and Times of Miguel de Cervantes*. My favorite scholarly sources are the original novel in Spanish and the English translations, in particular the 2005 translation by Edith Grossman.

I wrote *Miguel's Brave Knight* to show how the power of imagination can be a great source of comfort and hope in times of struggle and suffering.

—M. E.

Illustrator's Note

I met Cervantes's Don Quixote (*Don Quijote* in Spanish) during my senior year in high school. For weeks on end, our enthusiastic teacher shared and discussed passages from the book that read like an epic comedy. I didn't truly appreciate the genius of it all until much later.

When I was asked to illustrate *Miguel's Brave Knight*, I charged into it like a knight facing giants.

The best thing was that it gave me an opportunity to read the story in Spanish once again. Creating the images while reading the book was one of the most enlightening pleasures I've ever had.

Of course I did a bit of research, including the "casual" encounter with a 1968 Cervantes bio by American Heritage Press with dozens of notes and pictures. Not to mention Margarita's wonderful words! The prints by Gustave Doré also served as inspiration. Pen and ink and watercolor seemed to be the way to go for the illustrations. I hope you agree.

—R. C.

Historical Note

Cervantes lived during a significant time in European history. This was the era of improved mapmaking, the exploration of the New World, and the colonization of the Americas. It was the age of many advances in science: both Copernicus and Galileo were active during Cervantes's lifetime. Only a hundred years before Cervantes was born, Gutenberg had invented a printing press with moveable type, and by 1500, great quantities of books were being printed throughout Western Europe. In the arts, Leonardo da Vinci and Michelangelo were producing masterpieces in Italy and William Shakespeare was hard at work on his plays in England.

Biographical Note

Engraving by Frederick Mackenzie

Miguel de Cervantes Saavedra was born in Alcalá de Henares, Spain, in 1547. His father, an impoverished descendant of minor nobility, was a vagabond barber-surgeon who regularly squandered his money on gambling. He was jailed twice for failing to pay his debts. The family had to move often, fleeing the collectors. Young Miguel attended school when he could. In Madrid, he studied with Juan López de Hoyos, who had four of Miguel's poems published.

At the age of twenty-two, Miguel wounded a man in a duel and had to flee Spain to avoid severe punishment. Two years later, he and his brother Rodrigo enlisted in a naval expedition and Miguel was wounded in a sea battle against the Turks. They were then captured by pirates and sold into slavery in Algiers. Several efforts to escape failed, but finally relatives in Spain raised enough ransom money to free Rodrigo, while Miguel remained a captive for several more years. When he was finally freed, Miguel returned to Spain, where friends were surprised by his lack of bitterness. Instead of seeking revenge, he spoke in favor of peace.

Miguel secured a job purchasing food for the Spanish navy. He traveled the country listening to stories told by farmers, hunters, innkeepers, beggars. When an error in the official navy account book led to his arrest, he ended up in the same debtors' prison where his father had been held. Once again Miguel found refuge in stories, imagining the adventures of an elderly bookish knight. After his release, he composed a lengthy manuscript called *El ingenioso hidalgo don Quijote de la Mancha (The Ingenious Gentleman Don Quixote of La Mancha)*. Written in the language of the common people, it was the first book in Western literature that depicted an imaginative character in the real world. It was published in 1605, and within a year, figures from the story were becoming folk heroes.

Miguel de Cervantes died in April 1616, just a few days before the passing of William Shakespeare. Don Quixote, the knight he created, is still a beloved character worldwide.

Don Quixote, A Cultural Icon

Miguel de Cervantes is widely regarded as the creator of the first modern novel. *The Ingenious Gentleman Don Quixote of La Mancha* is one of the most influential books in Spanish and Latin American culture, and the fictional knight has exerted an enormous influence on Western culture. Since the appearance of the book in 1605, it has inspired a multitude of artworks—not only drawings, paintings, and sculptures, but also books, poems, plays, operas, ballets, and films.

In the nineteenth century, noted artists Honoré Daumier and Gustave Doré produced illustrations of this fictional character's adventures. And in the twentieth century, Pablo Picasso's paintings of the wistful knight became some of the most familiar images of Don Quixote in modern art.

Don Quixote is such a well-known international figure that his idealism has even become part of the English language. Visionary acts of hope are known as "quixotic deeds."

Illustration by Gustave Doré

Bronze sculpture by Lorenzo Coullault Valera in Madrid

Painting by Pablo Picasso